Oh, Brother

Kathy Mallat

BEETS

TOMATOES

Walker & Company
New York

For my brothers, "Jimmy-don't" and Dan

First published in the United States of America in 2003 by Walker Publishing Company, Inc.

Published simultaneously in Canada by Fitzhenry and Whiteside, Markham, Ontario L3R 4T8

For information about permission to reproduce selections from this book, write to
Permissions, Walker & Company, 435 Hudson Street, New York, New York 10014

Library of Congress Cataloging-in-Publication Data

Mallat, Kathy.
Oh, brother / Kathy Mallat.
p. cm.
Summary: A young rabbit's older brother teases her by stealing her blanket, but also proves that he loves her.
ISBN 0-8027-8875-0 — ISBN 0-8027-8876-9 (RE)
[1. Brothers and sisters—Fiction. 2. Blankets—Fiction. 3. Rabbits—Fiction.]
I. Title.
PZ7.M29455Oh 2003
[E]—dc21   2002193373

The artist used Van Gogh oil pastels, Prismacolor permanent markers, and Prismacolor colored pencils
on 16-ply Crescent illustration board to create the illustrations for this book.

Book design by Bruce McMillan

Visit Walker & Company's Web site at www.walkerbooks.com
and Kathy Mallat at www.kathymallat.com

Printed in Hong Kong
10 9 8 7 6 5 4 3 2 1

Baby loves her blankie.

She also loves her brother.

He is kind to Baby. . .

except when he teases.

"Brother, don't," says Baby.

But Brother does.

"Brother, *don't*," insists Baby.

But Brother does.

"Brother, *don't,*" demands Baby.
But Brother does.

"Brother, don't," yells Baby.

But Brother does.

"Oh, no. Oh, Brother."

"Brother, don't!" cries Baby.

But Brother does.

He is kind to Baby. . . .

well, most of the time.